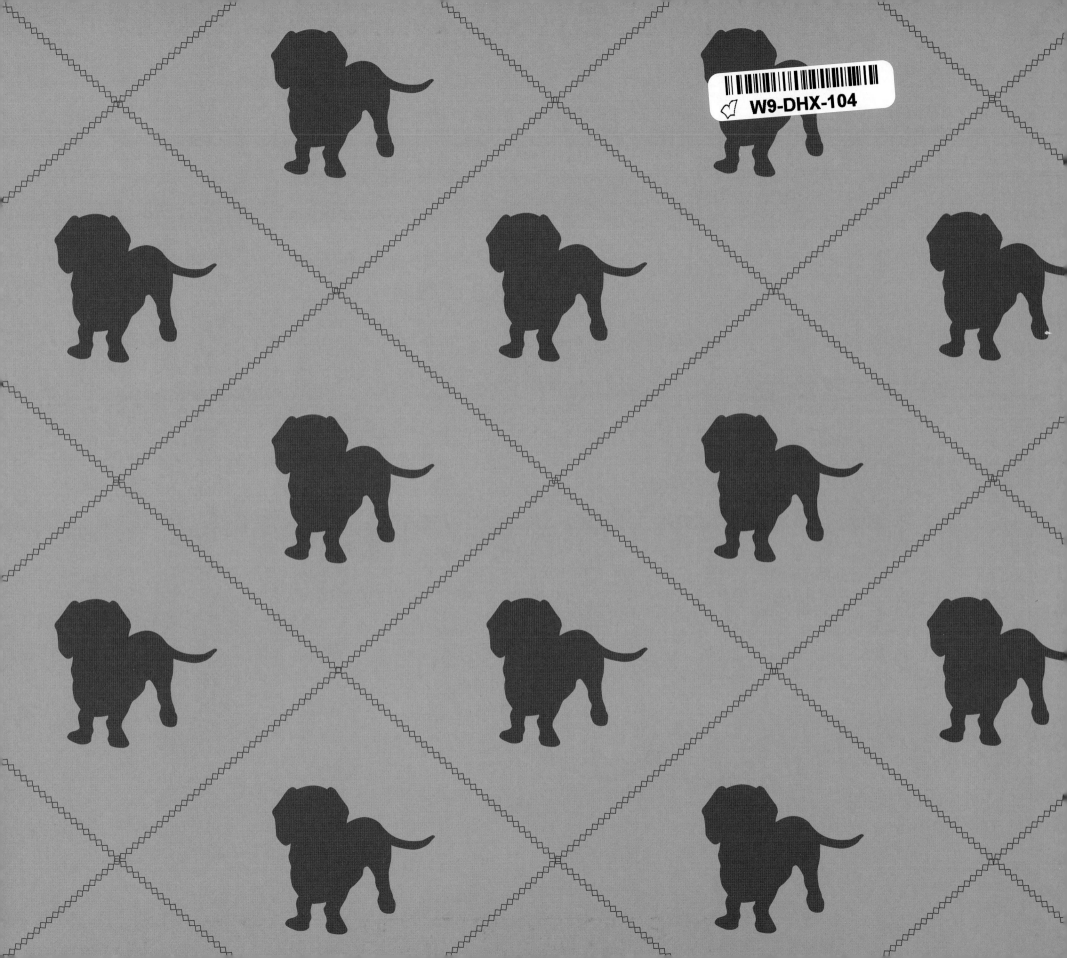

For Judson and Beford, my space camp buddies.

Special thanks to Richie Swann, Anna Evans, Randy Sr. & Randy Jr.,
Jay Upchurch for the great star photos, and the good people at Artist &
Craftsman Supply, who keep me knee-deep in construction paper!

Published by Underdog Endeavor Productions, LLC. Charleston, SC
Printed by Pacom in South Korea

Fifth Edition, printed 2023

ISBN - 10: 098195233X
ISBN - 13: 978-0-9819523-3-8

For more information please go to:
sammydogbooks.com

The ADVENTURES of SAMMY

the Wonder Dachshund

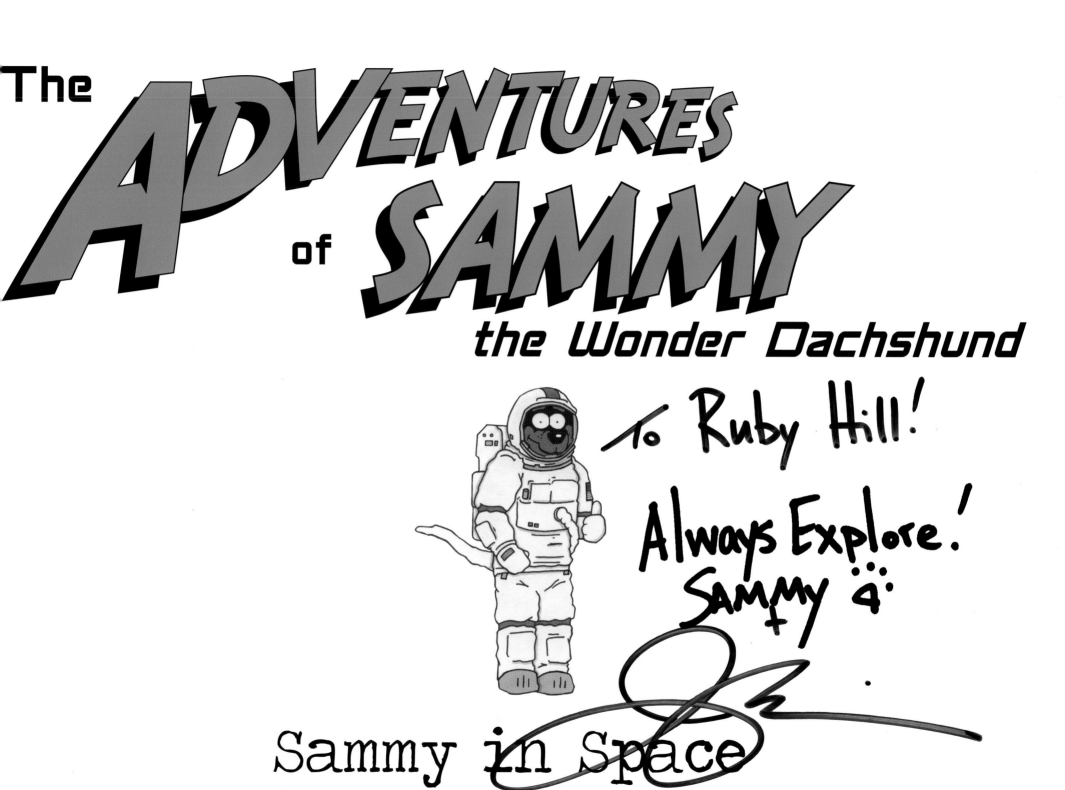

To Ruby Hill!
Always Explore!
Sammy 🐾

Sammy in Space

Story and Illustrations by Jonathan D. Miller

It was early in the morning, but Sammy couldn't wait to get to work.

He was very excited, because his company was announcing some big news!

"The Internet has been full of debate about whether or not Pluto meets the definition of a planet," explained Sammy's boss. "One of you will go into space to make observations, so we can settle this once and for all."

"We've thought long and hard, and Sammy, you have been selected for the job!"

Sammy couldn't believe it! Ever since he was a puppy, he dreamed of traveling to space. He began to think back on the summers he spent at space camp with his friends.

He remembered playing astronaut at his house...

"Sammy!" shouted his boss, bringing him back to the present. "This won't be an easy task."

"Normally it takes future astronauts 20 months to go through training, but you need to be ready in three weeks!"

"You'll have to get into shape, train hard, and study a lot."

"Report to NASA's Astronaut Training Program first thing in the morning!"

Sammy got to NASA and couldn't wait to begin. As he walked down the hall, he stopped to take a look at all the brave animals that had gone into space before him. He knew he had his work cut out for him.

ANT

TURTLE

KANGAROO

MOUSE

FISH

WORM

GUINEA PIG

MONKEY

FROG

FRUIT FLY

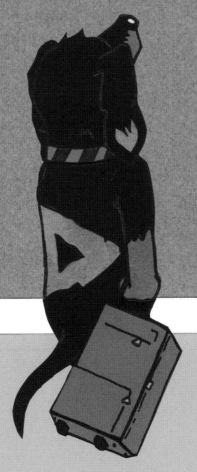

Sammy would have to go through flight school so he could fly planes and know what to do if any problems came up.

On his first day, Sammy learned to use a parachute.

He had to prepare for his mission by studying for hours and hours and hours!

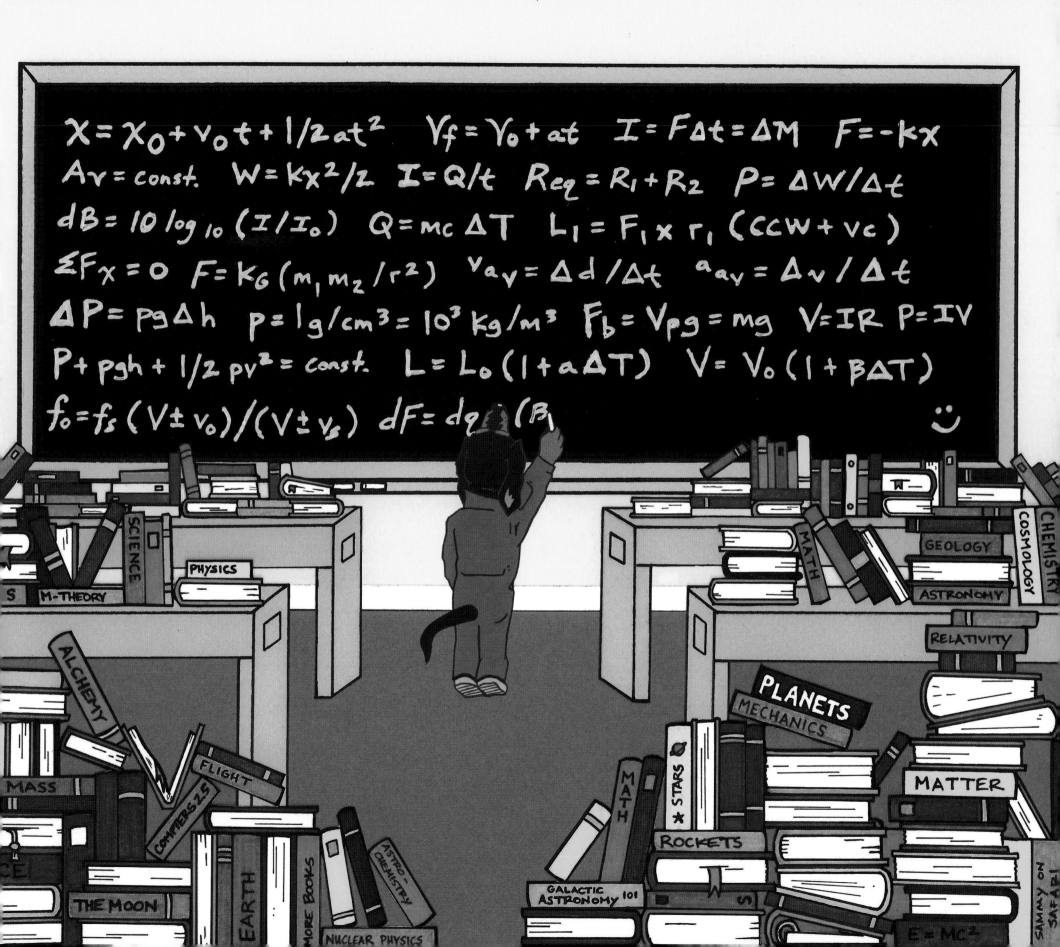

At the end of the week, Sammy was ready to fly a plane on his own.

Next came Sammy's survival training. He learned how to build a shelter, start a fire, and use maps in case of a crash landing.

After Sammy made it back from the wilderness, he rode in the "Weightless Wonder." It was a large plane that flew in a special way, making Sammy float like he would in space.

Sammy had to learn how everything in the space shuttle worked.
This took some time, but he caught on quickly.

After more tests, Sammy was fitted for his space suit. He was starting to feel like a real astronaut!

Sammy had to get used to wearing his space suit. He got into a huge pool and practiced doing tasks underwater, so he'd know how it would feel in space.

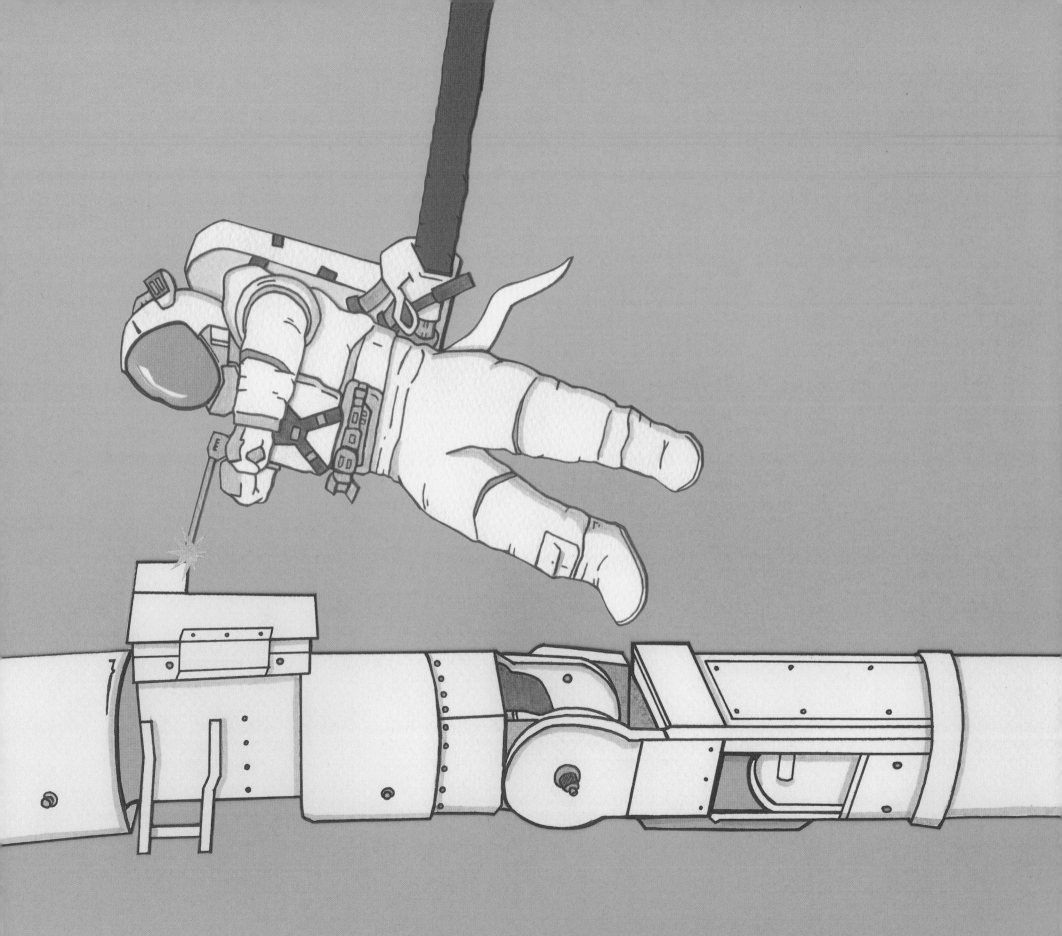

Then the big day came. Sammy couldn't believe it!

As he sat in the shuttle on the launch pad, he thought about the hard work he went through to get there.

And then the countdown began.

3... 2... 1...

LIFT OFF!!!!!!!!!

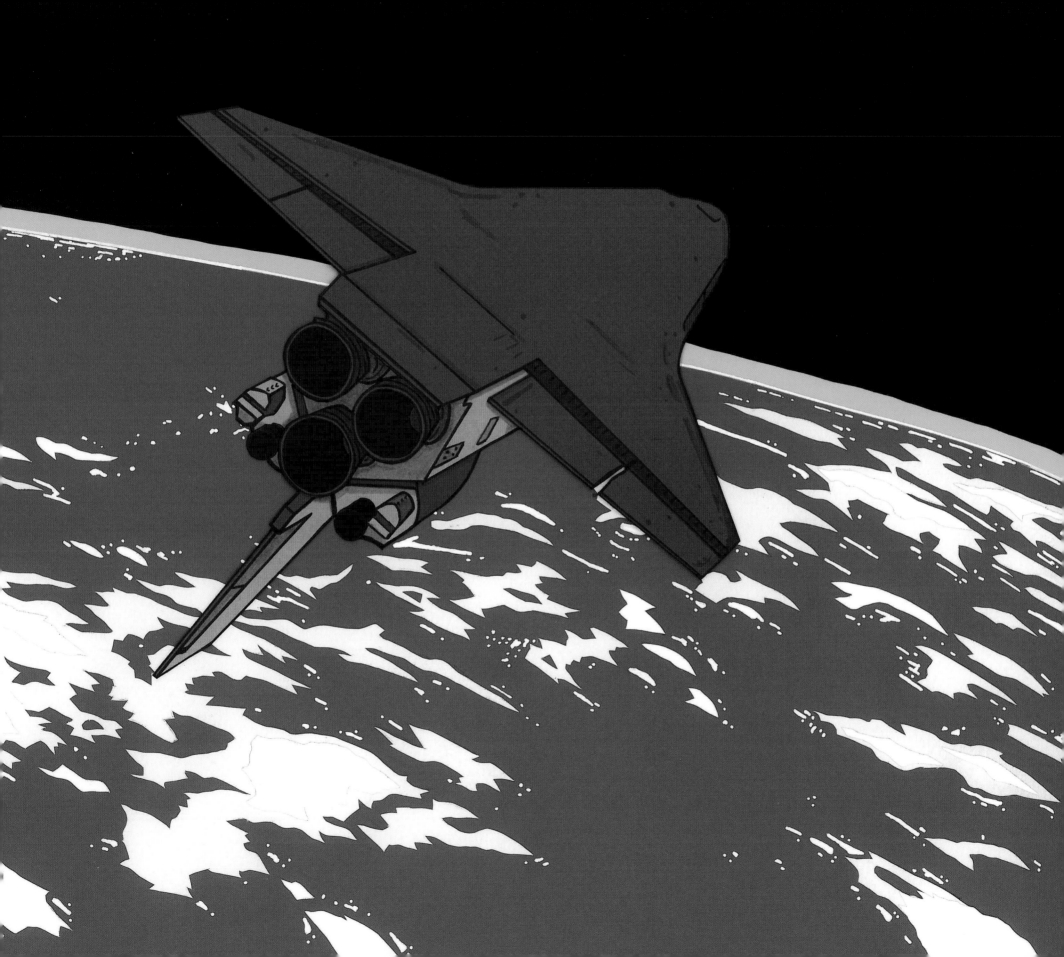

The first stop on Sammy's mission was the International Space Station, where he met with astronauts from around the world.

He was able to look at and collect data from some of the closest planets in the solar system.

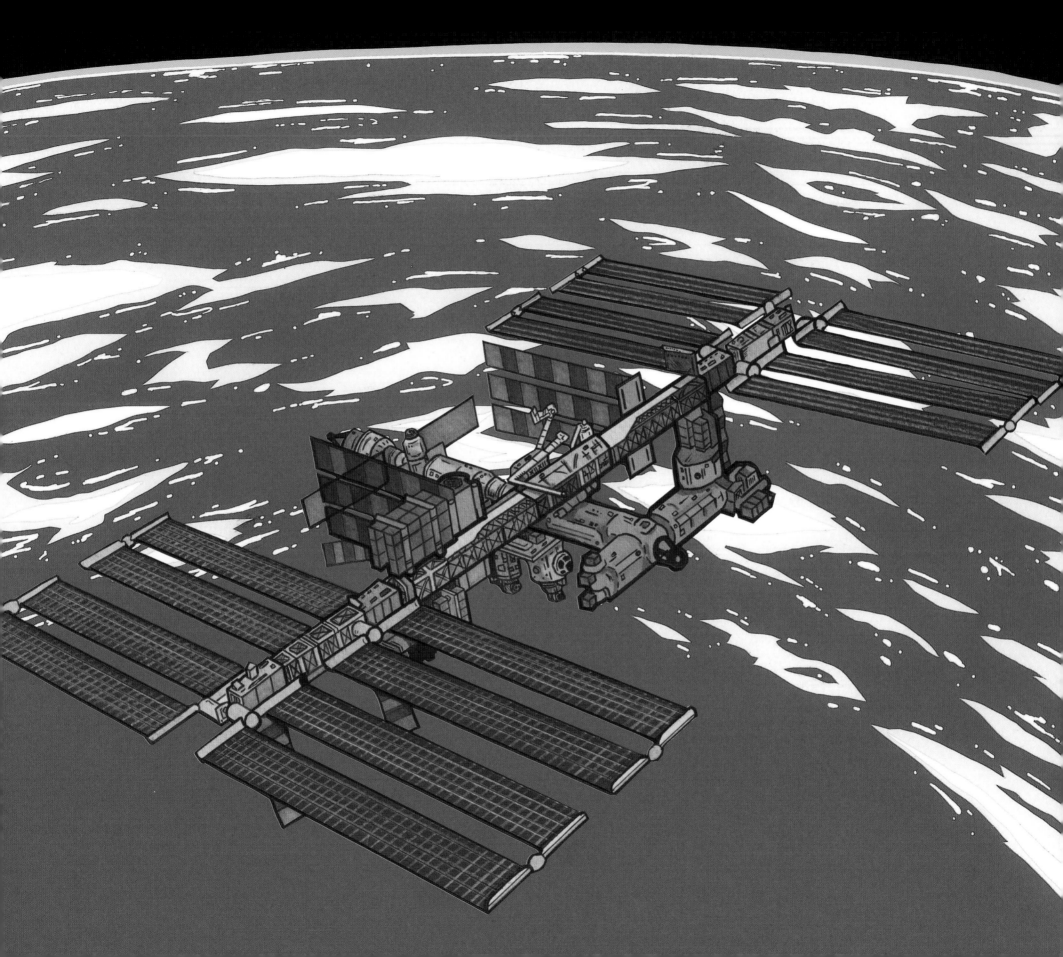

He saw and measured the smallest planet, Mercury.

He viewed the clouds of Venus - the hottest planet!

Sammy looked at Mars, called the "Red Planet"
because it is covered in rusty dust.

Sammy left the space station for a quick walk on
the moon before he went to get a closer

look at the other planets.

From the shuttle, Sammy observed our largest planet, Jupiter.

He flew around the rings of Saturn.

Sammy saw the planet that spins on its side, Uranus.

Then Sammy saw the stormy planet of Neptune.

And finally Sammy got close enough to examine Pluto.
He was surprised by what he found!

With his research finished, it was time for Sammy and the crew
to head home to Earth.

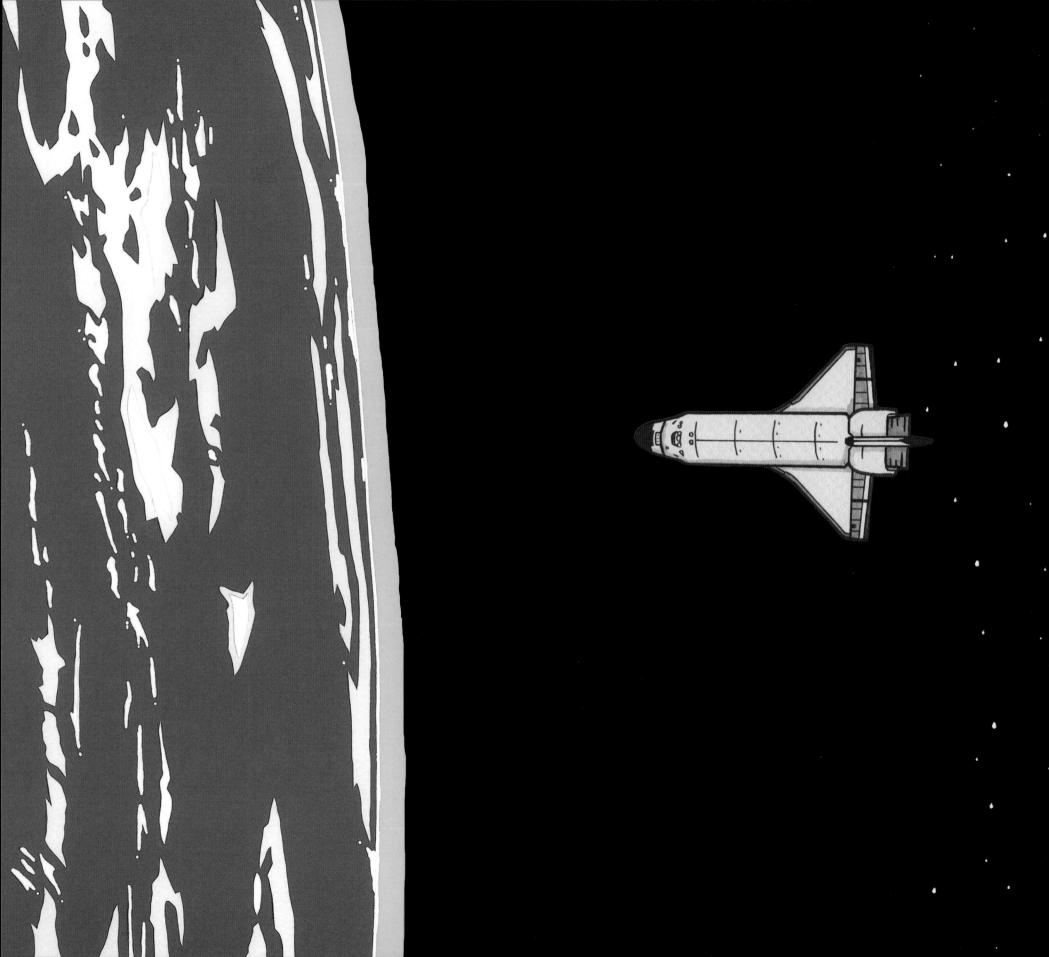

Sammy arrived home to cheers and pats on the back.

He was awarded a gold pin for his first flight into outer space.

The next day, Sammy turned in his final report. He concluded: "Pluto's size affects its gravitational pull in relation to its orbital zone. It will have to be classified as a 'dwarf planet.'"

"Wow, that is literally the smartest thing I've ever heard! Another job well done, Sammy," said Sammy's boss. "We've got big plans for you in the future. Now go home and get some rest."

That night, Sammy decided to sleep under the stars. As he fell asleep, he thought about his training and trip to space. He realized some of our dreams may be as big as the stars, but with enough hard work, time, and dedication, anything is possible.

Illustrator's Note:

All the illustrations in The Adventures of Sammy the Wonder Dachshund series are made by layering cut-out pieces of colored construction paper and card stock. These shapes are arranged to form a much bigger picture and then are given a little detail with the use of a Sharpie marker. It takes an average of 30 to 40 hours to construct each page.

Here is a simplified example of the process:

I hope you enjoy the pictures as much as I loved making them. -Jonathan D. Miller

See more artwork at sammydogbooks.com.

If you want to read about Sammy's other adventures, get a copy of Sammy's Last Week in Charleston, Sammy on Safari, or Sammy's Family Tree Vol. 1 today!

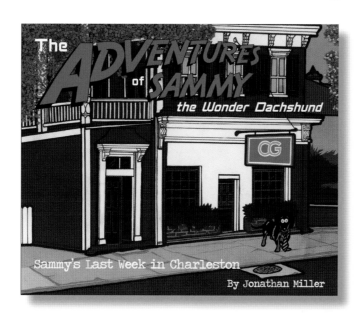

sammydogbooks.com